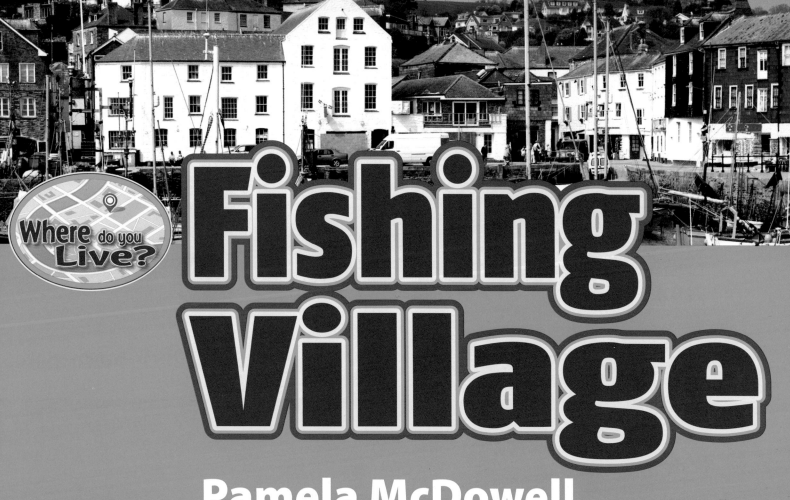

Where do you Live?

Fishing Village

Pamela McDowell

www.av2books.com

LET'S READ
AV²
BY WEIGL™
ADDED VALUE • AUDIO VISUAL

Go to **www.av2books.com**, and enter this book's unique code.

BOOK CODE

W649569

AV² by Weigl brings you media enhanced books that support active learning.

AV² provides enriched content that supplements and complements this book. Weigl's AV² books strive to create inspired learning and engage young minds in a total learning experience.

Your AV² Media Enhanced books come alive with...

Audio
Listen to sections of the book read aloud.

Video
Watch informative video clips.

Embedded Weblinks
Gain additional information for research.

Try This!
Complete activities and hands-on experiments.

Key Words
Study vocabulary, and complete a matching word activity.

Quizzes
Test your knowledge.

Slide Show
View images and captions, and prepare a presentation.

...and much, much more!

Published by AV² by Weigl
350 5th Avenue, 59th Floor New York, NY 10118
Website: www.av2books.com

Library of Congress Cataloging-in-Publication Data

McDowell, Pamela.
 Fishing village / Pamela McDowell.
    pages cm. -- (Where do you live?)
Includes bibliographical references and index.
 ISBN 978-1-4896-3605-8 (hard cover : alk. paper) -- ISBN 978-1-4896-3606-5 (soft cover : alk. paper) --
 ISBN 978-1-4896-3607-2 (single user ebk.) -- ISBN 978-1-4896-3608-9 (multi-user ebk.)
1. Fishing villages--Juvenile literature. I. Title.
GT5904.M33 2015
307.76--dc23
                          2015013480

Printed in the United States of America in Brainerd, Minnesota
1 2 3 4 5 6 7 8 9 0 19 18 17 16 15

072015
072415

Project Coordinator: Jared Siemens
Design: Mandy Christiansen

The publisher acknowledges Alamy, Corbis Images, Getty Images, iStock, and Shutterstock as the primary image suppliers for this title.

Fishing Village

CONTENTS

I live in a fishing village.

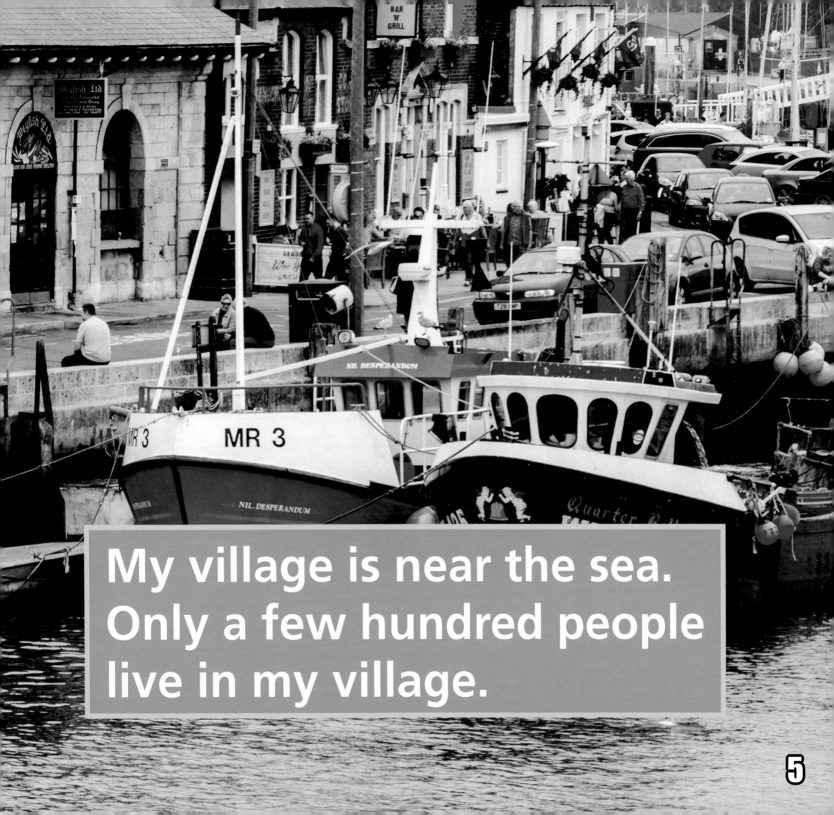

My village is near the sea. Only a few hundred people live in my village.

5

My fishing village has a tall building called a lighthouse.

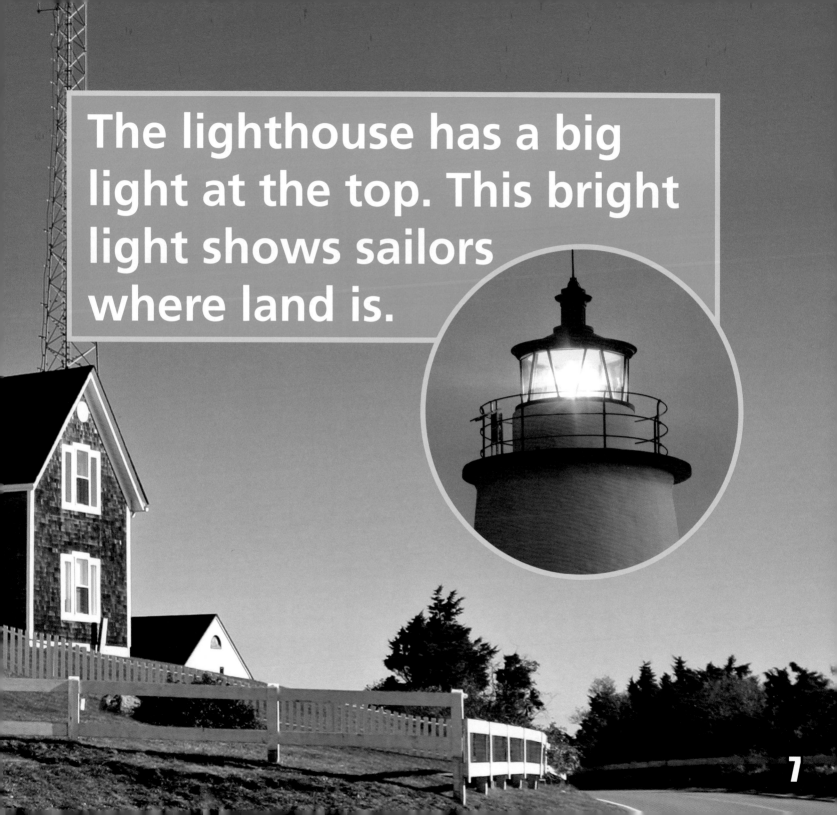

The lighthouse has a big light at the top. This bright light shows sailors where land is.

My home is a small house next to the sea.

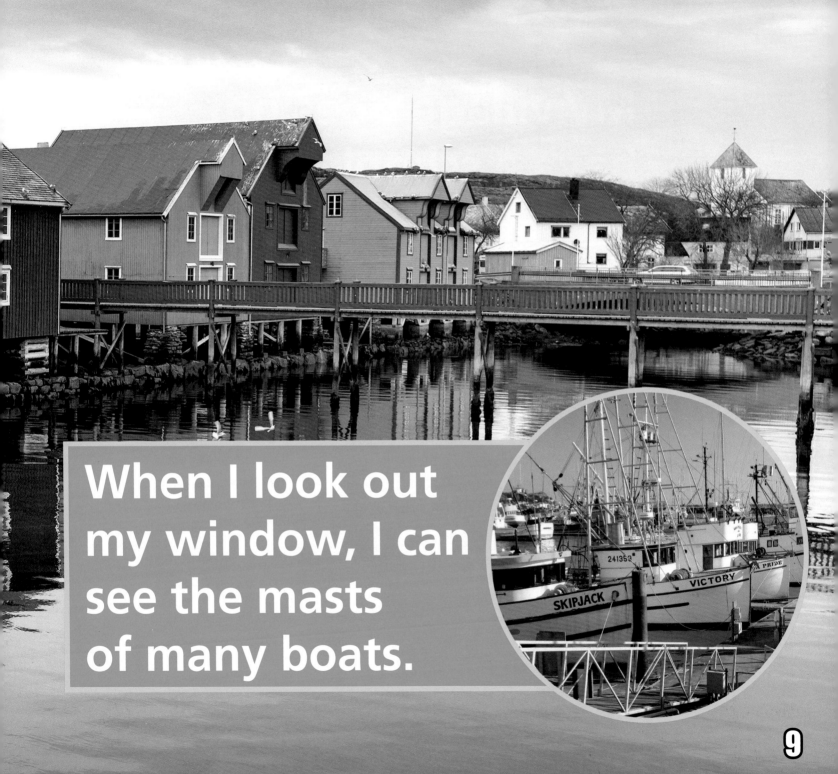

When I look out my window, I can see the masts of many boats.

My village does not have a school.

I take a boat and a bus to get to school each day.

People often use boats to go places.

Boats in my village are many different sizes. Some are used for work and some are used for travel.

Most of the fishing boats are tied up at the dock.

The dock is a busy place where people meet and work.

Fishers catch many kinds of seafood.

I like the crabs they catch.

My village has fun places to go and things to do. I can fish from the dock and play on the beach.

I like to look for seashells in the sand with my friends.

19

The people in my village vote for our leader.

The leader of a village is called a mayor.

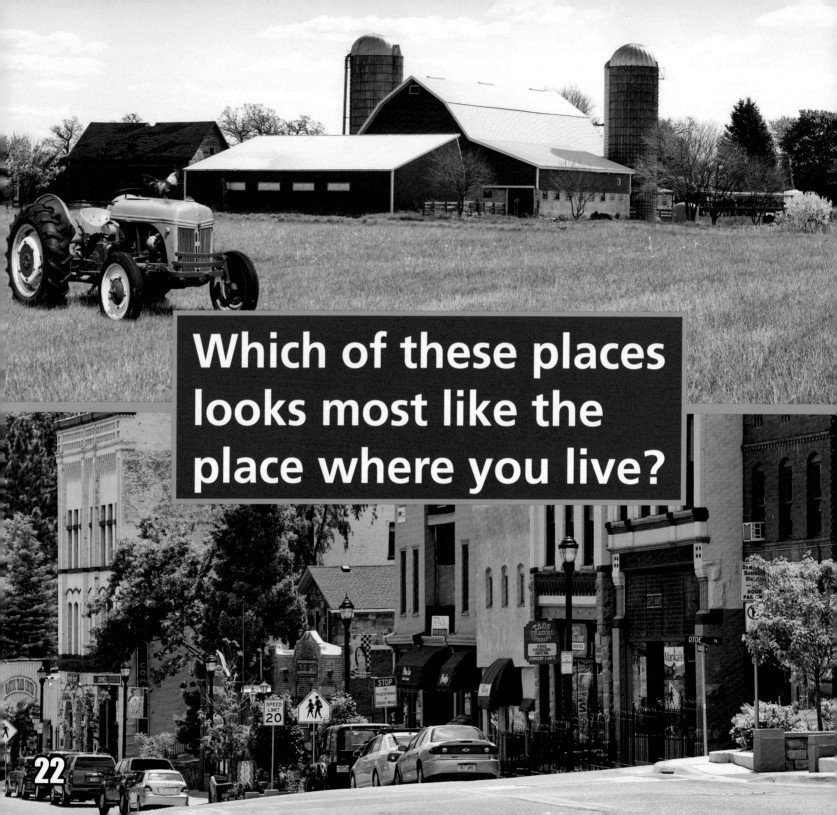

Which of these places looks most like the place where you live?

What is the same?
What is different?

23

KEY WORDS

Research has shown that as much as 65 percent of all written material published in English is made up of 300 words. These 300 words cannot be taught using pictures or learned by sounding them out. They must be recognized by sight. This book contains 62 common sight words to help young readers improve their reading fluency and comprehension. This book also teaches young readers several important content words, such as proper nouns. These words are paired with pictures to aid in learning and improve understanding.

Page	Sight Words First Appearance
4	a, I, in, live
5	few, is, my, near, only, people, sea, the
6	has
7	at, big, land, light, shows, this, where
8	home, house, next, small, to
9	can, look, many, of, out, see, when
10	does, have, not, school
11	and, day, each, get, take
12	go, often, places, use
13	are, different, for, some, work
14	most, up
16	kinds
17	like, they
18	do, from, on, play, things
19	with
20	our

Page	Content Words First Appearance
4	fishing village
6	building, lighthouse
7	sailors, top
9	boats, masts, window
11	bus
13	sizes, travel
14	dock
16	fishers, seafood
17	crabs
18	beach
19	friends, sand, seashells
20	leader
21	mayor

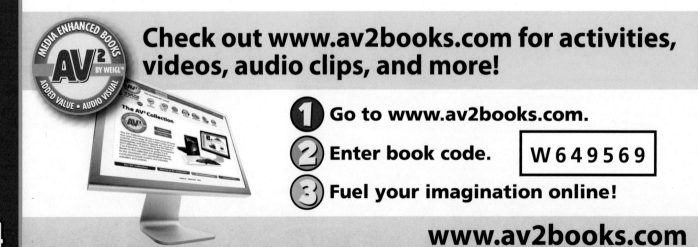